BY R.A. MONTGOMERY

A DRAGONLARK BOOK

Illustrated by: Keith Newton
Book design: Stacey Boyd, Big Eyedea Visual Design
For information regarding permission, write to:

CHOOSECO
P.O. Box 46
Waitsfield, Vermont 05673
www.cyoa.com

A DRAGONLARK BOOK

ISBN: 1-933390-38-7
EAN: 978-1-933390-38-3

Published simultaneously in the United States and Canada

Printed in the United States.

0 9 8 7 6 5 4 3 2 1

Produced in cooperation with the World Anti-Doping Agency.

WWW.WADA-AMA.ORG

For Ramsey

A DRAGONLARK BOOK

READ THIS FIRST!!!

WATCH OUT!
THIS BOOK IS DIFFERENT
than every book you've ever read.

Don't believe me?

Have you ever read a book that was about YOU?

This book is!

YOU get to choose what happens next
—and even how the story will end.

DON'T READ THIS BOOK FROM
THE FIRST PAGE TO THE LAST.

Read until you reach a choice.
Turn to the page of the choice you like best.
If you don't like the end you reach, just start over!

YOU are an Elf! Yup! You are different from humans—those giants who live in the Upper World. They are 20 times bigger than elves; they have round heads and small ears! At least that's what your brothers and sister elves and the rest of the elves say. Humans are also scary.

You have big pointy ears, a pointy head, and are small, even for an elf. You are also very SMART. Some say that you are MAGICAL.

But, you are unhappy. An unhappy elf? How can that be? Elves are wonderful creatures who help humans in all sorts of ways, often do tricks and cause some mischief, and always fight against evil. So, why are YOU unhappy?

You decide to talk with your dad.

Turn to the next page.

You look at your dad and can barely hear him or see him because of the tears streaming down your face. He is a famous elf and has a big white beard.

"You are a great kid! Don't ever forget that. Your mom and I love you," he says.

You see the warmth and the love in his eyes and hear them in his voice. But you are hurting.

"Dad, nobody wants me. I'm always picked last for games, or plays, or clubs—anything. I'm a flop." You continue to blubber.

"Pick something nobody else does and be really good at it. It could be flying butterflies, it could be surfing rainbows, it could be making truly magical hats."

"Thanks, dad," you reply. You're not sure if that was helpful or not.

If you decide to pretend that you have truly magical talents and have done truly magical things (you'll need to fib big time), then turn to page 4.

If you choose to really develop special skills like rainbow surfing, turn to page 7.

You decide that fibs—"little white lies"—are just the way to get recognized and liked. So, here goes!

All the younger elves gather every afternoon at the cream puff factory to eat leftovers, tell stories of their deeds in the Upper World and play Spoff—a three net, multi-ball game of great skill. You almost never get to play.

Screwing up your courage and tugging your hat down as tight as it will go—it is red and green and you are proud of it—you sit down for the cream puff eating and begin to spin tales of great derring-do and magical events that you have done in the Upper World.

Go on to the next page.

Nobody listens to you.

An elf named Rooppee shouts out, "I need five brave elves to travel to the Upper World right away."

"Why?" you squeak.

"Because the ugly-but-good humans are under attack from the Weed Things."

"Oh no, the Weed Things, that's terrible," several other elves murmur.

"I'll go!" you shout in your loudest squeak. "I fought the Weed Things with my special magic and won many times."

The other elves stare at you in awe and respect for the first time in your life. But it's a lie--what if they find out?

"I'll go alone. My magic is strong," you continue on, digging the hole for yourself deeper and deeper. You've never gone to the Upper World before.

"Yeah!! Yeah!!! Go forth!!" they all shout. Nobody wants to battle the Weeds.

If you make up an excuse and back out now, turn to page 14.

If you go to the Upper World, turn to page 12.

“Dad’s always full of great ideas; but he’s him and I’m me. What works for him might not work for me. But...I’ll give it a try,” you say to yourself. Sometimes you wish you were a human.

You spend the rest of the day avoiding other elves. Needing a quiet place to think, you sit under a giant mushroom and sip on a sarsaparilla soda. Yum!!!

“What to do? Surfing rainbows sounds cool. I’ve never done it, but who knows, maybe I’d be good at it. I like rainbows. As for butterflies...well, I don’t know. Could be cool. Yuck to making hats.”

Suddenly a figure creeps out of the bushes next to the mushroom.

Yikes!!! It’s a troll! Run!

Turn to the next page.

"Hey, no problemo, elfie! I won't bite, nope, not me. I'm a friendly troll."

"I've never heard of friendly trolls," you say, ready to run.

"Well, here I am. And I need an elf friend...like you. We can help each other."

You look at the troll with his hairy face, his yellow eyes, his round head, his bulbous body, and spidery arms. Uckyee!

"I can't help you. I can barely help myself."

"That's why I'm here, buckaroo. To help you, just you. You see, I know that you're always picked last. With my help that will be only a memory."

"How?" you ask, hopeful that the troll might actually help you.

"First, just call me Flippto. Deal?"

Go on to the next page.

You are intrigued by this ugly creature; remember, trolls are enemies of elves. You are playing with fire!

"OK, Flippto, deal. How can you help me be the best-ever rainbow surfer?"

Flippto looks at you as though he were measuring you for a new suit of elf clothing. He puts his skinny hand to his big, round jaw, squints, and after about 15 minutes, he says, "I have an answer and a proposition. Are you ready? Are you serious? Are you trustworthy?"

"Yes to all three!" you reply, surprised at your quick response. Flippto has grabbed your interest.

"Here's the deal," Flippto says. "I will provide you with undetectable magic to let you always—always—win. You will be Elf-world-famous for all time."

Turn to the next page.

"What do I have to do for you?" you ask.

"Ah, that is the question isn't it? Simple. When I am ready, I will ask you to do my bidding—whatever that might be. It could be in a month, a year, or never."

You are so desperate for success that you agree, before you even know what he means.

You shake hands with Flippto, a little nervous about what he might ask of you. But, a deal is a deal. Right now you are looking at Success.

The take-off point for rainbow surfing is just beyond the cream puff factory.

"Hold on!!!" A really tiny elf approaches you.

Go on to the next page.

"Don't make bargains with the devil," he says in a whisper and then runs off.

"Whoa, jellybean," you say to yourself. This is a warning.

If you decide to keep the deal with Flippto and ignore the tiny elf, turn to page 26.

If you decide to try and fly butterflies and ignore Flippto and his dangerous offer, turn to page 18.

When you think about it, lying or trying to be something you aren't never really works. You always get found out and then it is worse than before. So, you decide to really go to the Upper World. You might NEVER come back! The Weed Things are horrible, gobbling up everything they want. There is no stopping them. The humans hate them, but there is little they can do. They need the help from the elves. They have always needed elf help. You're it!

But—yikes!—you have no skills, you are a coward, you are scared...yet, you bragged! Well, it's now or never. Instead of being picked last, you pushed yourself to the head of the line for the trip upward. YOU picked yourself first. You had better win—or at least try.

Up you go, whistling to pretend you are brave, not concerned about the Weeds and used to this sort of thing.

Just before you get to the third rung of the ladder to the Upper World, you turn, wave to the others and, before you can stop yourself, say, "I'm scared!"

Turn to page 54.

"OK, OK! I'll go. Happy to go! Excited to go! Nothing like it! Those Weed Things are going to be sorry to see me again! But--before I go, I've got one thing to do, a must. Then I'm off to the Upper World. Any one want to join me?"

There is not a peep from any of the other elves. Who would want to go to fight the Weed Things? Of course you will never actually go, you'll just make up some great story. Who can prove you didn't go? No one!

On the other hand, if you can make a good excuse not to go, you will get the credit and none of the pain.

"My mom's sick, and I have to take care of her. If she is better, I'll go."

The other elves look at you and nod. 'Big talk, no action' is what they are thinking.

Turn to page 17.

Is getting help cheating?, you wonder as you trudge home to see your dad. You aren't sure. You decide to ask him. He'll give you a straight answer.

"Dad! Dad! Are you there?" you shout as you open the door.

No answer. You enter the living room. There is a note on the table that reads: GONE TO FIGHT THE TROLLS. LOVE, DAD.

Oh no, you moan. This could be dangerous for your dad. So, at that very moment you decide to go after him and help him. There is not a moment to lose.

Turn to page 52.

Too bad for you, your mom is gone on one of her famous trips. She travels the known world of the elves right up to the border of the trolls and goblins—dangerous areas where no smart elf ever goes.

Your mom, Trident of Light, as she is known, gives away the Gift of Kindness to all she meets. Small bags of buttered popcorn are her gifts. They are ginormously delicious and the bags never empty! They refill so that people who get them can give popcorn to all they meet and so on and so on.

Everyone knows Trident, so you can't hide behind her being sick.

Uh-oh! You'll have to go to the Upper World.

Maybe you could fake a broken leg. Then you won't have to go.

If you fake a broken leg, turn to page 25.

If you go to the Upper World, turn to page 30.

Yuck, you say to yourself. Trolls have been mean and the enemies of elves for years—skillions of years. You would betray your whole elf world to deal with a troll. Who knows what he would ask in return for helping you cheat your way to victory in the rainbow surfing.

So what if you are always picked last! You can be good at something...you hope. Why not try butterfly flying? But what is butterfly flying? You haven't the foggiest notion of what it is. Aren't you too big to climb on the back of a butterfly, even for an elf? Maybe there are giant butterflies that you know nothing about. Ginormous ones!!!

Turn to page 21.

English
Bulletin Parents User Agreement
WebKiddies
Photos
Directions
Fun Stuff
Enter Site

There is a weekly Elfnet posting of all sorts of things—Spoff game schedules, rainbow surfing contests, human movie showings, cream puff baking classes, troll protection lectures, and elf houses for sale. Also, you can post notes to all and ask help or request info on anything in the elf world. It's called Elfmail and it's run by Lila and Avery, two really cool elves.

Wowzer!!!! You don't have to look far to find it: Butterfly Flying Instructions and Contests. Contact Lila and Avery at Elfmail.

You do, and you are on your way!

Turn to page 22.

Lila and Avery meet you at the offices of Elfmail. They greet you with big smiles.

"You are one of the first elves—actually the ONLY elf—who has shown up for the butterflying instruction." Avery hands you a page of instructions and an entry form for the First Annual Butterflying Event in Elfdom.

Reading the instructions, you soon realize that the butterflying is a kite-flying event. You don't actually fly butterflies. You build a kite and get butterflies to be the tail of the kite. You are relieved. You really didn't want to climb onto a huge butterfly and 'fly' it.

"Great, but where do I find the butterflies and how do I get a kite?" you ask.

"It's up to you," they both reply, and dance away.

Nothing in the rules says you can't get help. If you decide to ask your dad for help, turn to page 15.

If you decide to search for the butterflies and build your kite by yourself, turn to page 33.

May
S M T W T F S
1 2
3 4 5 6 7 8 9
10 11 12 13 14 15 16
17 18 19 20 21 22 23
24 25 26 27 28 29 30
31 2009
January

JAM

"Ha, ha!" you chuckle to yourself. "No one will ever know that my leg is fine!"

You get a roll of star-spangled bandage from the medicine cabinet and two sticks of wood from the hearth by the fireplace for splints. You add a dash of raspberry jam to the bandage to make it look super real—just like blood!

All splinted up, you get the crutches your oldest brother used after he really broke his leg playing Spoff. Now it's off the cream puff factory to explain why you can't go to the Upper World, land of the giant humans.

Turn to page 51.

What do elves really know, especially tiny ones? you ask yourself. They have never been nice to you. So what if Flippto is a little bit creepy or edgy—he is offering you success! No one else has. You go for it.

"OK, Flippto, what's next?" you ask, swelling with confidence.

"See those other surfers, the ones by the popcorn fountain?" he asks.

"Yeah, so what?" you reply. You are getting cocky and smart-alecky now.

"Well, they are the best surfers. Any rainbow, anytime, and they surf them as if they were part of the rainbows. No falls. No slips. Perfection."

"So, what do I do?" you ask, beginning to lose your newly-found confidence.

Flippto grins, opens a small purple-and-red bag at his waist and…

Turn to the next page.

"Here is your magic weapon!" he says, handing you the bag.

"What is it?" you ask, dazed by the prospect of holding magic in your own hands.

"An invisible powder that, when blown toward the other rainbow surfers, will knock them off the rainbows. Simple and very effective. You win, you will be the hero, and no one will ever know how it happened—except for you and me."

Turn to page 46.

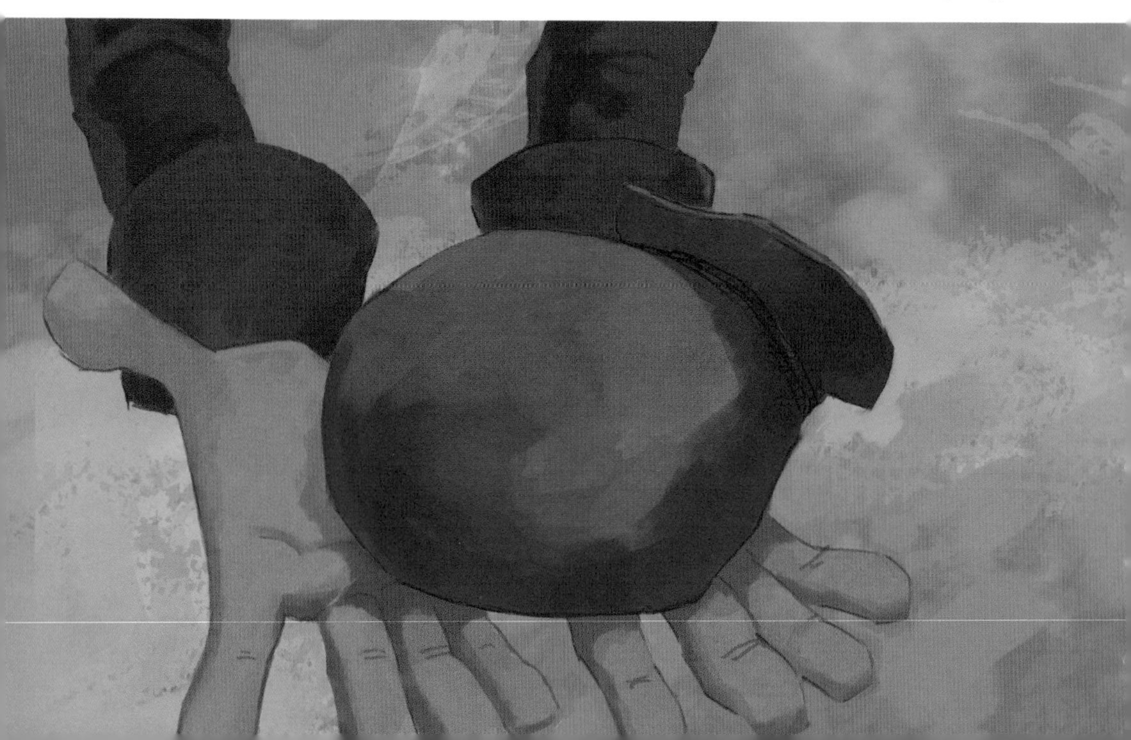

Too bad, it's too late to ask for help from Down Under. Or is it? Who whispered in your ear that it was too late?

You did. Lack of belief in yourself has always been a problem for you. You lose before you begin. Don't just give up—ask for HELP!

So, you whisper in your smallest voice, "Hey down there, can you hear me?"

"Of course! We are elves—we can hear everything all over the world at any time! Do you need help?"

"Yes," you reply. "How did you know?"

"Everyone needs help. It's just the way things are. We elves are all about help. So, we're on the way. We were just waiting for your call. Some are on the ladder already. Hang in there."

Twenty-three elves pour up out of the hole in the ground. They yell and shout and rush the Weed Things. The Weeds take one look at these elves and ZIPPO FOGO!!!! They are gone like a memory of a cold day.

"All ya gotta do is ask!" the lead elf says. "Don't wait until you are picked last. Speak up!"

The End

Something your dad said struck a bell in you. "I won't turn back!! I will succeed!" Brave words and thoughts indeed, but what lies ahead?

After what seems like a zillion days you pop out of the earth into the Upper World. Wowzer! It is beautiful up here; not as beautiful as your world down below, but great anyway. You like the trees, the houses, the mountains, the clouds, the lakes.

Suddenly, you spot them! Four humungous humans sitting around a table under a strange-looking tree. They spot you right away, too. Maybe because your ears are that sparkling orange-and-silver mess.

"Elf! Hey Elf! We need your help!" one of them shouts. "The Weeds are trying to destroy our farms and gobble everything up!" This human speaking is a really big man with giant arms, a pin-head, legs like tree trunks, and ears that look like wings.

"How can I help?" you squeak.

Turn to the next page.

"Well, elves can do magic, right?" the pin-head says. The others watch you, waiting for your answer.

"Umm...not really," you answer.

"But you always help humans, right?" ol' pin continues.

"Well, mostly. We do fix things for poor people, we do help the planet stay clean, we do try and sweep away bad thoughts from the 'nasties,' you know—the people who want more and more power and money." In your heart you want to do all these things you speak of. If only you could really help!

Turn to page 47.

"I'll do it all by myself," you announce to the sky and the trees and the world. There is no one to hear. Wait a minute. There is someone to hear your words. As a matter of fact, there are three ones to hear you.

"You need help? We'll help you. All you have to do is ask!" says the biggest elf kid you have ever seen.

"But it wouldn't be fair," you say.

"Who says?" he asks.

"I don't know; I just thought..."

"Well, we think it's fair. Everyone needs help. Let's go."

Turn to the next page.

The three elves are named Jasper, Ell, and Blooto. It takes all of the afternoon to round up eight friendly butterflies who agree to be the tail of the kite.

Now for the kite itself.

"We'll enter as a team," Blooto, the biggest elf says. "It'll be swell!"

Jasper has wood for the frame, Ell has paper for the kite skin, and Blooto has string and glue.

Turn to the next page.

You design the kite. You are really good at it and the other elves really like what you design.

Finally the great day arrives. You and the other elves bring your giant orange, purple, and green kite to the flying ground. Your butterflies come along flying around you. There are 32 other teams, and hundreds of elves who came to watch.

That day you and your team win the silver medal for butterflying! You are the proudest elf in all the land of Elfdom.

Good for you. Fair and square wins the day. You'll never be picked last again.

The End

You hold the purple-and-red magic bag in your grimy hand. "NO! I won't!" you say to yourself, placing the bag behind a lollipop bush by the side of a lemonade pond. You hope Flippto doesn't see it.

With fear and pride your two companions, you mount a large rainbow and copy the position of the other rainbow surfers. They wave at you and smile.

"Hey, dude, welcome. Surf's up! Let's do it!" the medium-sized elf next to you says, dropping into a standard rainbow surfing crouch.

Unbelievably, you stand up and surf the rainbow like a pro! You do it! No magic, no deal with the devil, no feeling like you are always picked last. Do it!! Do it!! It's your own magic.

The End—or maybe the beginning.

A super big rainbow comes sliding into view and there are four others right next to it. All the surfer elves jump on rainbows. You get the big one. But you are not scared. Flippto the troll has assured you of success. No more "picked last" for you. The magic purple bag will take care of all that.

You curl your toes on the edge of the rainbow and drop into the crouch just like the others. Whoosh!!! What a thrill! Two of the other surfers wave at you and give you big thumbs-up signs.

Suddenly, you slip and just manage to hold on. Where is Flippto when you need him? Then you remember the purple bag.

Go on to the next page.

The purple bag!!! The key to success. It's right there, hanging from your belt. Go ahead, open it!

When you open the purple bag a cloud about the size of your fist emerges, dances before your very eyes and speaks in a slupopery voice, "Oh, Great Elf, tell me what I must do."

"Win!! I want to win!!" you answer.

"Throw me at the others. You will win." The cloud has spoken.

Turn to the next page.

The little cloud works. All the other surfers fall off their rainbows and YOU win!!! You are the champion of the elf world!

That night there is a huge party for you at the cream puff factory. All the elves join in to celebrate your victory in the rainbow surfing competition. Things are going well, really well. But...an elf you have never seen before approaches you.

"Hey, champ, it's me, Flippto. Remember me? It's payback time." Flippto is dressed in an elf disguise, and you fear what he is about to ask.

"What do you want?" you whisper.

"Simple, I want you to let 32 trolls into the elf world. That's not too much to ask, now, is it?" He snickers in a nasty way.

Thirty-two trolls in the elf world will destroy the peace of your world. You will betray your fellow elves!!!!!

Turn to page 45.

Before you have a chance to do anything, the rainbow surfers you knocked off their rainbows straggle into the party. They are bruised, two have broken arms, one a broken leg. Bandages cover their faces. They all shout, "That elf is a traitor!!" They are pointing at you.

"Am not!" you reply.

"Are too!" they all shout back.

Flippto sneaks away; he knows the jig is up.

The truth of what you have done comes out. Not only the use of the purple bag and its cloud powder, but your betrayal of all elfdom to the trolls is revealed.

You are the biggest loser in all of elf history!

The End

"What happens when they fall off their rainbows?" you ask, a little scared.

"Don't ask, don't tell." Flippto smiles a deadly smile and looks away.

"You mean they—"

"Don't ask, it's our little secret." Flippto sniggers a bit like a cat turning a purr into a puke.

If you climb on a rainbow without the magic bag, turn to page 39.

If you take the magic bag with you and hop the next 'bow, turn to page 40.

"Right! That's what we need right now. Help to fight the nasties who sent the Weeds to overpower us so they can take over our part of the world." He looks at you as though you were some kind of special being like an angel or a minor god. But you're not, you're just an ordinary elf who is always picked last.

You are surprised to hear yourself say, "OK, I'll help. I'll do my best." But what can you really do?

If you dig down deep into your elf self and find the power to help the humans, turn to page 48.

If you decide to ask for help from the other elves Down Under, turn to page 29.

"Help me! Help me!" you plead to any unknown Elf Power available. "Now is the time. Right now! Help me!!!"

You never really believed in magic, but suddenly you feel a flow of energy that lifts you up and makes you enormous and strong and brave. All the things you never thought you were you now are.

"Where are those Weeds?" you ask in a voice that demands respect. "Let me at them!"

The humans point toward a tulgey* forest over a hill. You FLY there—something you didn't even know you could do—and before your eyes you see a band of Weeds—green, ugly, wiry, and mean.

Raising your arms above your head, you cast a cloud of yellowish vapor over the Weeds. It stuns them and leaves them weak and confused. They retreat, a defeated force, no longer a threat!!!!

You did it! No tricks! No fibs! Just you! Congratulations! You'll never be picked last again!

The End

** The tulgey wood is a made-up place Lewis Caroll invented in his poem "Jabberwocky."*

You limp on your crutches to the cream puff factory. Seven elves are sitting in the shade of a strawberry tree, because the sun is so strong it would melt the cream puffs in a flip of a dip.

"Hi, gang!" you cry out, "I'm wounded. See?! I came across a troll who sneaked across the border last night to rob the pozza delivery truck. ('Pozza' is the elf word for a pizza-like food made with worms instead of anchovies and raspberry jelly instead of tomato sauce.) I beat him all the way back to Trollville, but he broke my leg! Sorry, I can't go to the UPPER World."

No one says anything and they all turn their backs to you.

"Hey, elves, how about a 'thanks' or something?" you say, beginning to get nervous.

The smallest elf named Mackie speaks up.

"Not true. Not true at all. I followed you to your house and saw you put on the bandage and splints. You didn't fight any troll. Liar, liar, pants on fire!!"

That certainly didn't work. No, sirree! Back to the drawing board. No cream puffs for you today. You'll get picked last or not at all for now. Why not try a different choice?

The End

The border between Trolldom and Elfdom is a tulgey wood and a briar patch. Elves get lost in the woods and stuck forever in the briars.

"Dad! Dad!" you yell in your loudest elf squeak.

No reply. You push on into the tulgey wood.

There he is! Surrounded by five grizzly trolls breathing green fire and spitting yellow slime.

"Run! Leave me! Save yourself! I love you!" your dad yells.

Without thinking, you throw yourself at the trolls and, with a mighty effort, beat them off!!! You, always picked last, win the day! What a grand elf you truly are.

You and dad make your way home, and your dad tells the story far and wide of the day YOU saved his life by singlehandedly beating off the trolls in the tulgey wood.

The End

All the elves look up at you, their eyes wide open in amazement. You have spoken the truth, the truth that they all feel and know. They are all scared. All of them.

Rooppee, the biggest of the elves, speaks out. "The truth has been spoken! This is the bravest elf to admit what we all feel. We must help!"

Go on to the next page.

"Yes, we will all go to the Upper World. We will join together and defeat the Weeds!!"

A giant cheer goes up, and you feel the love and acceptance of your fellow elves. Up all of you go, up the ladder to the Upper World! Good luck!

Three days later you ALL return from the ginormous fight against the Weeds in the Upper World. You won, but the cost was high. Three elves were captured, two were badly wounded, but the day was won! The humans salute you!

The End

ABOUT THE ILLUSTRATOR

Illustrator Keith Newton began his art career in the theater as a set painter. Having talent and a strong desire to paint portraits, he moved to New York and studied fine art at the Art Students League. Keith has won numerous awards in art such as The Grumbacher Gold Medallion and Salmagundi Award for Pastel. He soon began illustrating and was hired by Walt Disney Feature Animation where he worked on such films as *Pocahontas* and *Mulan* as a background artist. Keith also designed color models for sculptures at Disney's Animal Kingdom and has animated commercials for Euro Disney. Today, Keith Newton freelances from his home and teaches entertainment illustration at the College for Creative Studies in Detroit. He is married and has two daughters.

ABOUT THE AUTHOR

AT THE TEMPLE OF LITERATURE AND NATIONAL UNIVERSITY
(VAN MIEU-QUOC TU GIAM) IN HANOI, VIETNAM

R. A. MONTGOMERY has hiked in the Himalayas, climbed mountains in Europe, gone scuba diving in Central America, and worked in Africa. He lives in France in the winter, travels frequently to Asia, and calls Vermont home. Montgomery graduated from Williams College and attended graduate school at Yale University and NYU. His interests include macroeconomics, geopolitics, mythology, history, mystery novels, and music. He has two grown sons, a daughter-in-law, and two granddaughters. His wife, Shannon Gilligan, is an author and noted interactive game designer. Montgomery feels that the generation of people under 15 is the most important asset in our world.

For games, activities, and other fun stuff, or to write to R. A. Montgomery, visit us online at CYOA.com